Wallace & Gromit IN THE WRONG TROUSERS

NICK PARK

BBC CHILDREN'S BOOKS

It was a day like any other day.

Wallace enjoyed having a lie-in most mornings, so Gromit, as usual, was the first one up. He fetched the paper from the doormat and went into the kitchen, boiled the kettle, made a pot of tea and poured himself a cup. It wasn't until he went to cross off the day on the calendar that he remembered today *wasn't* like any other day at all. It was his birthday!

Gromit was looking at his watch, wondering when Wallace was going to get up, when he heard the postman at the front door. Running into the hall he skidded to a halt. Five letters; four brown envelopes, all for Wallace, and a green one for Gromit. He took them back to the breakfast table, stepping neatly over the 8.45 goods train as it made its way round the house on the Double-O track, and opened his letter. It was a musical card from Wallace and it beeped an electronic 'Happy Birthday' at him.

Wallace may have forgotten to get up, but Gromit was glad he hadn't forgotten what day it was.

'TO A DEAR DOG'

Closing the card, Gromit heard the loud rasp of the buzzer on the wall. A red light by the word 'Breakfast' was flashing. Wallace must have woken up.

'It's my turn to have breakfast made for me this morning, Gromit!' he called. 'I'd like a three-minute egg and . . .'

Without waiting to hear any more, Gromit leaned over and pulled a lever down. *His* turn for breakfast? Had Wallace forgotten what day it was, after all? A complicated arrangement of pulleys swung into action as Wallace's bed was tipped up and he plummeted through a hole in the floor.

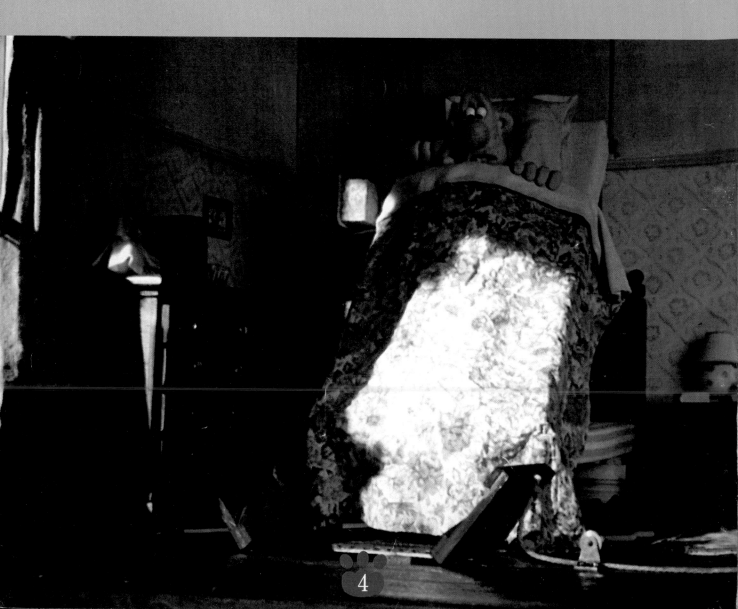

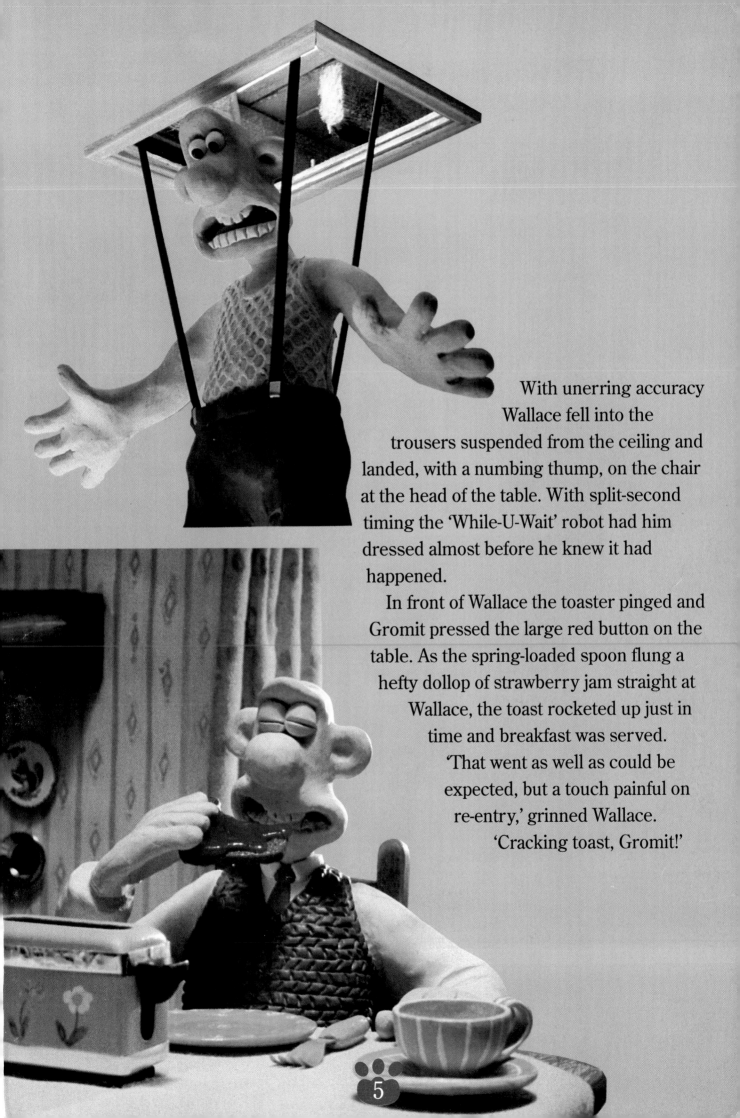

With unerring accuracy Wallace fell into the trousers suspended from the ceiling and landed, with a numbing thump, on the chair at the head of the table. With split-second timing the 'While-U-Wait' robot had him dressed almost before he knew it had happened.

In front of Wallace the toaster pinged and Gromit pressed the large red button on the table. As the spring-loaded spoon flung a hefty dollop of strawberry jam straight at Wallace, the toast rocketed up just in time and breakfast was served.

'That went as well as could be expected, but a touch painful on re-entry,' grinned Wallace.

'Cracking toast, Gromit!'

'Any . . . ah . . . post was there, perchance?' enquired Wallace, pretending not to notice the birthday card on the table. Gromit handed over the four brown envelopes without looking at him.

'Oh dear, bit steep . . .' muttered Wallace, opening the envelopes. 'They're all bills!'

Still ignoring the card, Wallace studiously examined his post. 'We shall have to economise, Gromit,' he said, getting up and going to his wall safe. 'I'll have to let the spare room out,' he went on, as he counted out three lonely coins. 'Look at that! I'm down to my last few coppers, and those presents weren't cheap either – oops! Well, Gromit, let's see what's on the 9.05, shall we?' added Wallace, with a silly grin on his face.

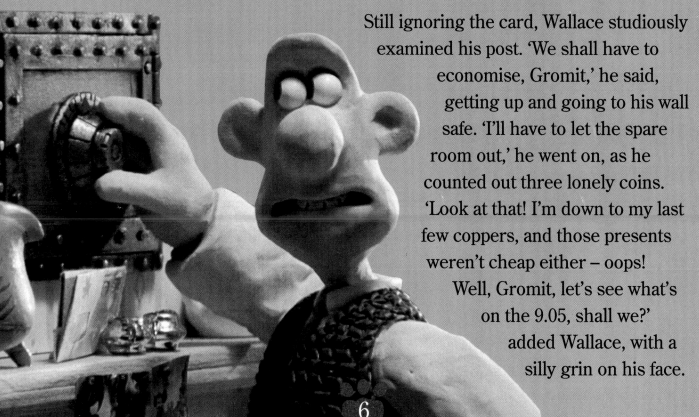

Right on time the train came chuffing through the door. As it passed Wallace, he bent down and grabbed from the last carriage a pink parcel, all tied up with gold ribbon. 'I wonder what this can be?' he said.

Gromit was dumbfounded when he discovered that he'd been given a matching collar and lead set.

'Happy birthday, chuck!' Wallace patted Gromit on the head and then put the collar round his neck. 'I knew you'd like it – you look like somebody owns you now – and that's just the first part!'

Wallace got up and walked out into the hall. 'Come and look in the front room,' he said, beckoning. Gromit followed, and as he stepped through the doorway he came to a dead stop.

He shrank back against the wall as the largest pair of gift-wrapped legs he had ever seen walked towards him and stopped right in front of him.

'I think you'll find this present a valuable addition to our modern lifestyle,' said Wallace, undoing the wrapping paper. 'They're Techno-trousers, ex-NASA, fantastic for walkies!'

Wallace tied one end of the lead to the Techno-trousers and clipped the other end to Gromit's new collar. He then punched some buttons on the control panel and pushed a lever up.

'There we go!' he turned to Gromit. 'Ten minutes' walkies coming up!'

To Gromit
Love
Wallace.

Gromit was unceremoniously dragged down the hall and out of the front door. Number 62 West Wallaby Street disappeared into the distance as the Techno-trousers marched Gromit down the road.

But before they had reached the park, Gromit slipped his collar and 'borrowed' a toy dog on wheels. The Techno-trousers were left happily walking round with the toy dog in tow, while Gromit enjoyed himself playing on the slide.

Meanwhile back at Number 62, Wallace was not enjoying himself. Whichever way he added up all the figures they didn't make a very comforting sum. 'It's no use prevaricating about the bush,' he sighed. 'We're going to *have* to rent that spare room out . . .'

By the time Gromit and the trousers arrived home, there was an advert in the front window. 'ROOM TO LET, APPLY WITHIN' it read, and it wasn't long before there was a ring on the door bell.

'I wonder who that can be?' Wallace put down his cup of tea and went to answer the door. Gromit carried on knitting. He wasn't sure how he felt about having a lodger in the house. Above the clicking of his needles he could hear Wallace asking whoever it was to come in. 'I'm asking twenty a week,' he said, as he began to go upstairs.

Gromit looked up. A small penguin, carrying a suitcase, was staring at him with a look that made him drop at least a dozen stitches.

'Do you like kippers?' asked Wallace as he and the penguin reached the landing. 'I'm partial to a nice black pudding myself – with bacon of course!'

They went past Gromit's room and Wallace opened the next door along the hall. 'It's a bit *dingy*,' he said. The penguin looked at him. A picture broke the silence by falling off the wall. 'But it's surprising what a lick of paint'll do, isn't it?'

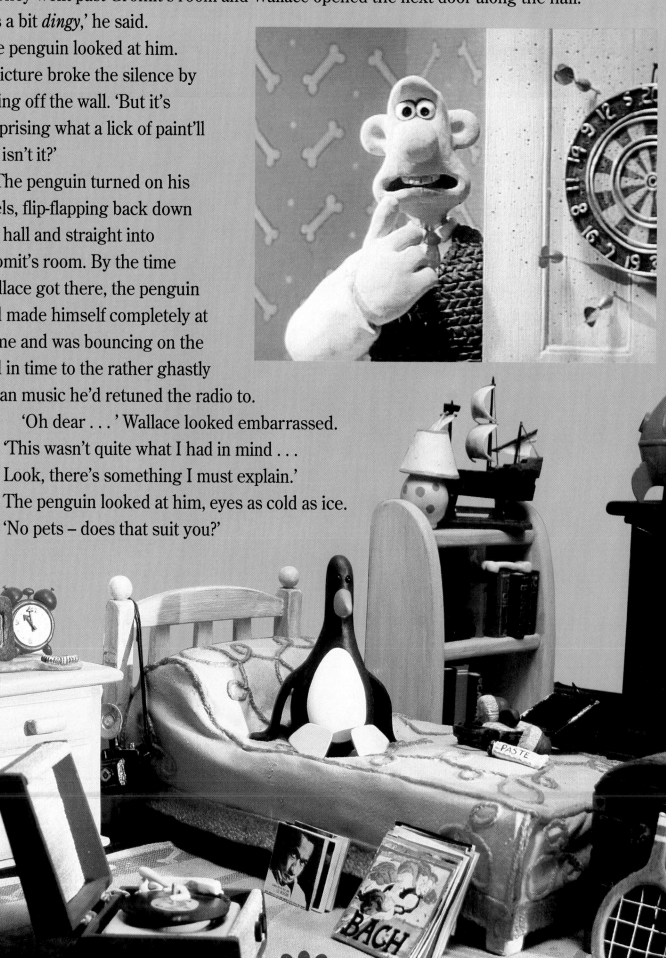

The penguin turned on his heels, flip-flapping back down the hall and straight into Gromit's room. By the time Wallace got there, the penguin had made himself completely at home and was bouncing on the bed in time to the rather ghastly organ music he'd retuned the radio to.

'Oh dear . . . ' Wallace looked embarrassed. 'This wasn't quite what I had in mind . . . Look, there's something I must explain.' The penguin looked at him, eyes as cold as ice. 'No pets – does that suit you?'

It suited the new lodger only too well. Later that day, after buying some more rolls of Gromit's favourite wallpaper, Wallace set to work redecorating the spare room for Gromit.

Gromit meanwhile had discovered that the feet of the Techno-trousers had a powerful suction grip. He was hanging upside down, repainting the ceiling of his new room, when he saw the penguin staring at him again. It was most unnerving.

Gromit's first night in his new room was horrible. Not only was it cold and unfriendly, but it was also noisy. The penguin still had *his* radio tuned to the station with the loud, jaunty organ music. Gromit hated it. Even when he moved downstairs onto the sofa the penguin's music echoed round him. Giving up the unequal struggle, Gromit admitted defeat and went outside to his kennel where he slowly sobbed himself to sleep.

The next day was no better. The penguin was everywhere, hogging the bathroom, bringing Wallace his slippers, picking up the newspaper first and, to add insult to injury, getting himself invited to dinner.

That evening as Gromit watched the two silhouettes in the dining room window, he knew there was only one thing left for him to do: leave home. He wrapped his brush, alarm clock and favourite bone in a hanky, and tied it to a stick. Then, dressed in his sou'wester and mackintosh, he gave Number 62 one last sad glance, wiped a tear from his eye and left.

Watching from a darkened bedroom, the penguin rubbed his wings together. He took a book entitled *Electronics for Dogs* off the shelves, then picked up an electric drill.

As thunder rumbled ominously outside, the penguin set to work on some rather radical adjustments to the Techno-trousers.

Next morning Wallace awoke a happy man with no idea what the day held in store for him. He was about to reach for the 'Breakfast' button, when the bed mechanism sprang to life.

'What's happening?' he cried out, as the bed tipped up and he fell through the hatchway in the floor. Instead of his nice pair of dark brown corduroys and a seat at the breakfast table, something else waited down below. 'It's the *wrong* trousers!' he said in amazement. 'And what have you done with the controls, Gromit?'

The controls weren't there and neither was Gromit, and no matter how loud Wallace yelled, nothing could stop the Techno-trousers as they took Wallace for an exhausting early morning walkies all over town.

Having spent a miserable night on the streets, Gromit was peering dejectedly at the 'Rooms To Let' notices in the newsagent's window, every one of which specified *No Dogs*. He didn't notice Wallace and the trousers leaping down the High Street behind him. His attention had been caught by a police notice.

There was a £1,000 reward offered for Feathers McGraw, who was the strangest-looking chicken he'd ever set eyes on. Gromit felt sure he'd seen the chicken somewhere before, but couldn't for the life of him think where. Shrugging, he walked off down the road.

As Gromit roamed aimlessly through the streets, not even bothering to look where he was going, Wallace suddenly appeared out of nowhere.

'They're the wrong trousers, Gromit – and they've gone *wrong*!' he yelled as the robotic legwear dragged him out of sight. 'Stop them! They've gone haywire! Help!' Gromit blinked in amazement, hardly believing what he'd seen. Then, out of the corner of his eye, he noticed something move in a nearby builder's yard. It was the penguin, and hanging round his neck, in a neat little box, was the control panel from the Techno-trousers. Something was definitely up, he thought as he watched the penguin go after Wallace.

Sitting in a café at the end of West Wallaby Street, Gromit waited. Eventually his patience was rewarded when he saw the penguin walk past the window. Throwing some money on the table, Gromit left the café and followed the mysterious bird until he stopped, checked he was alone and went down an alleyway next to the City Museum.

Hiding first behind some dustbins, and then a little nearer in a cardboard box, Gromit cut some eyeholes and watched as the penguin made notes and took some measurements. For one horrible moment, as the bird turned to leave, he seemed to look straight at Gromit, and Gromit thought he was going to be discovered. But the penguin just frowned and walked off.

Using every short-cut he knew, Gromit raced back to Number 62. It was almost as if he'd never lived there. Even the dog-flap in the back door had been replaced by a penguin-shaped one. Tip-toeing upstairs he went into his old bedroom and switched on the desk lamp.

In front of him he saw some plans for the City Museum which showed the layout for a diamond exhibition. So *that* was what the penguin was up to, thought Gromit.

Just then he heard the door flap swing to and fro. Switching off the light, he scuttled out of the bedroom and went to hide in the only place he could find – under the duvet where Wallace lay, still in the Techno-trousers, sleeping off his morning exercises.

Peeking out, Gromit saw the penguin coming down the hall wearing a red rubber glove on his head. *Now* he knew why he'd recognised the escaped criminal in the 'Wanted' poster! The lodger and the chicken were one and the same person! Gromit was stunned by Feathers McGraw's cunning disguise.

Feathers proceeded to put a big red crash helmet on Wallace's head and punched some commands into the control panel. The Techno-trousers took their sleeping passenger off down the stairs, and out into the street. Gromit knew he had to do something . . .

The whole town was asleep. The only things up and about were the Techno-trousers. While Wallace slept like a baby, they marched to the silent electronic commands from the control panel held by Feathers.

Going straight to the alleyway by the City Museum, Feathers activated the suction shoes and, climbing on board, walked the Techno-trousers up the wall to a second-floor window ledge. There he got off and sent Wallace on his way up to the roof and across to a large ventilation duct. Working from the notes he'd made, Feathers directed the Techno-trousers to their final destination – the diamond exhibition!

Suspended from the ceiling, with Wallace hanging like some strange chandelier, the trousers stomped through a display of dinosaur skeletons and into a room protected by a dazzling array of buzzing laser beams. Breaking one of those, Feathers knew, would set alarms ringing from here to a long prison sentence.

Sweat began to pour off the penguin as he manoeuvred the trousers above the diamond, and opened twin doors in Wallace's helmet. A three-pronged pincer spiralled down and made a grab for the main exhibit – the Blue Diamond. The pincers missed . . . missed again . . . and then got it! But at that point a ceiling tile came loose and one foot of the trousers lost its grip. The pincers and their precious cargo swung wildly in the air and broke a laser beam.

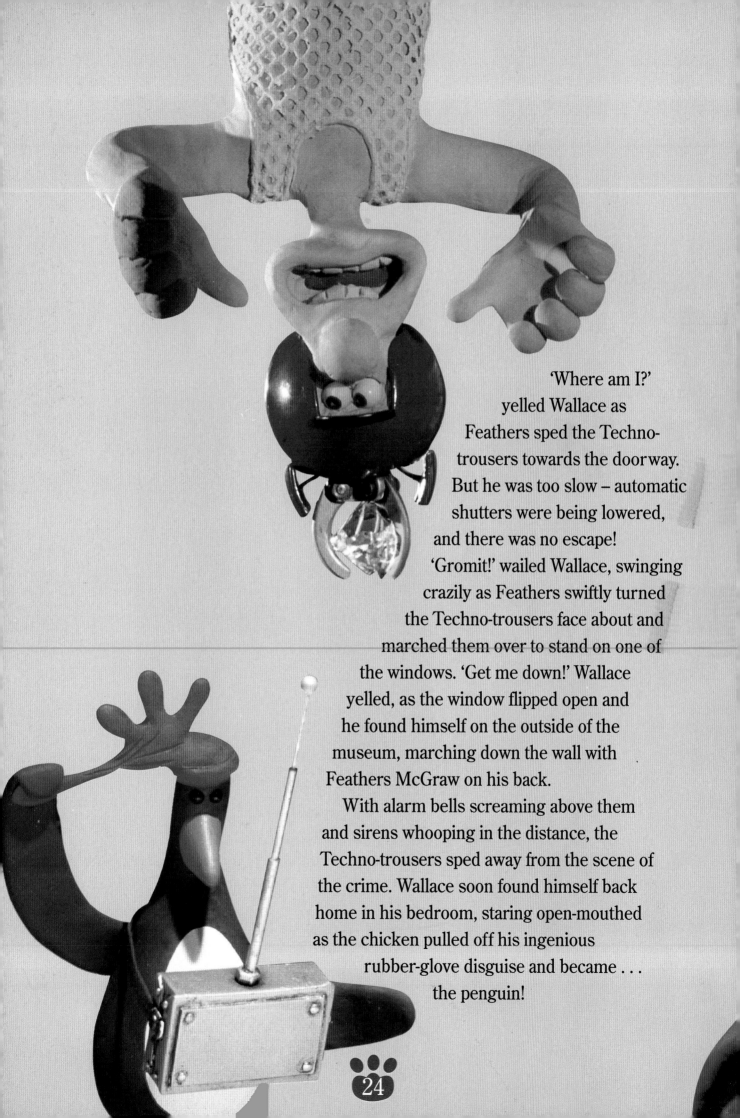

'Where am I?'
yelled Wallace as
Feathers sped the Techno-
trousers towards the doorway.
But he was too slow – automatic
shutters were being lowered,
and there was no escape!
'Gromit!' wailed Wallace, swinging
crazily as Feathers swiftly turned
the Techno-trousers face about and
marched them over to stand on one of
the windows. 'Get me down!' Wallace
yelled, as the window flipped open and
he found himself on the outside of the
museum, marching down the wall with
Feathers McGraw on his back.
With alarm bells screaming above them
and sirens whooping in the distance, the
Techno-trousers sped away from the scene of
the crime. Wallace soon found himself back
home in his bedroom, staring open-mouthed
as the chicken pulled off his ingenious
rubber-glove disguise and became . . .
the penguin!

'Good grief – it's you!' said Wallace, struggling to get out of the Techno-trousers. But before he could do anything, Feathers steered him into a wardrobe and slammed the door. 'Steady on will you – this piece of furniture's nearly new, you know!'

Feathers took off the control panel from around his neck and put the Blue Diamond in a sack. As he turned to leave the room, he found Gromit blocking his path, holding a large rolling pin in one paw and tapping it on the other in a very threatening manner. It looked like it was all over for Feathers, until he drew a revolver . . .

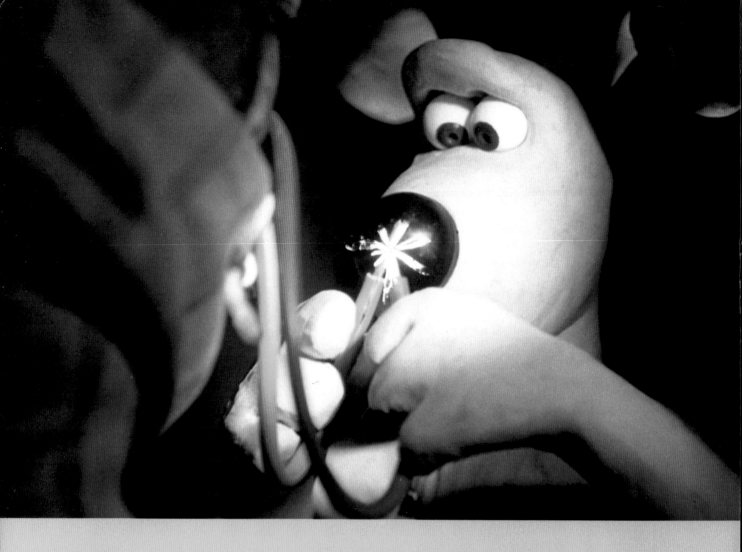

Gromit dropped the rolling pin and Feathers locked him in the wardrobe with Wallace. 'This is a fine how-do-you-do isn't it, Gromit?' Wallace looked at Gromit as he took the panel off the front of the Techno-trousers and short-circuited a couple of wires. The Techno-trousers began to stamp up and down. 'Crikey, Gromit – this'll ruin the woodwork,' complained Wallace, as the wardrobe parted company with its base and began to advance on Feathers.

'There goes my knotty pine!' moaned Wallace. The wardrobe shuddered as it hit a wall and its door burst open. Gromit leapt out after Feathers, but the penguin was too quick for him, jumping on to the banister and sliding downstairs. Flying off at the bottom, he landed on the coal tender of a passing express train.

Behind him Gromit heard Wallace yell for help, and he turned to see the wardrobe crashing towards him down the stairs. Jumping for all he was worth, Gromit found himself clinging to the hall ceiling light. Feathers took aim with his gun and fired.

The bullet missed Gromit, but cut through the flex above the lampshade. Gromit landed on the back of the train, which was making straight for the back door. Feathers was going to escape!

Just in time, Gromit flicked a passing switch which sent the engine curving round a bend in the track and he began to inch his way up the carriages. The chase was on.

Wallace, dazed from his fall downstairs, stepped out of the wardrobe and found himself standing in the last truck of the train. 'I'm right behind you, Gromit!' he called. Bullets ricocheted off Gromit's lampshade helmet as Feathers tried to rid himself of his pursuers.

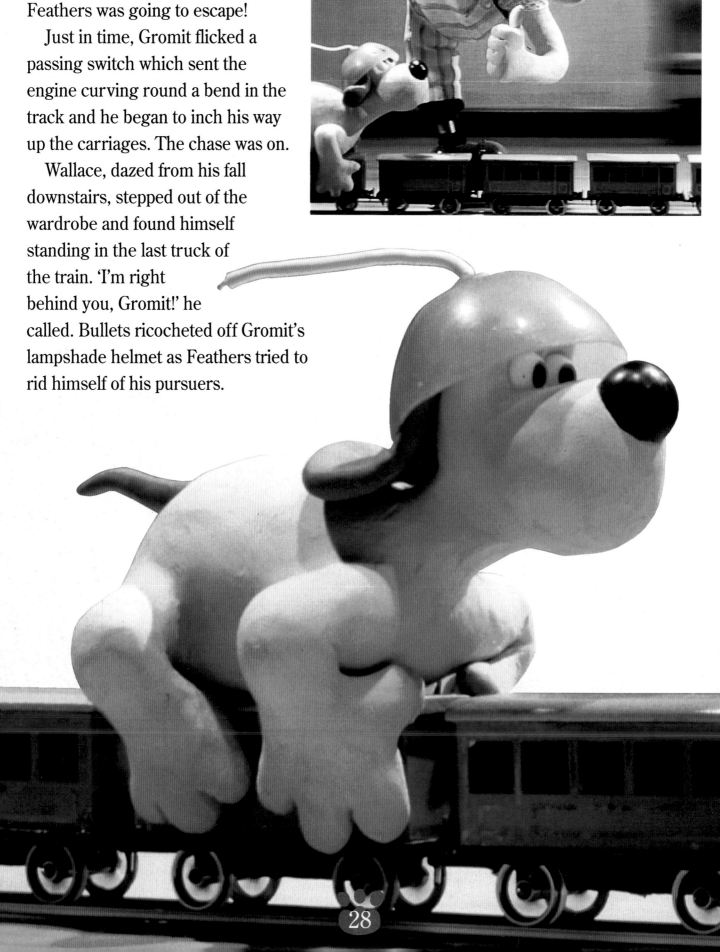

The next thing Wallace knew, his truck had jumped rails and was speeding up a parallel track and overtaking the dastardly penguin. Wallace grabbed the bird's gun and promptly hit a wall, pitching through a hatchway into the kitchen, leaving the Techno-trousers behind. He rejoined the chase on a vegetable trolley, grabbing a butterfly net on the way.

'Leave it to me, Gromit!' yelled Wallace, speeding by. But the net caught a passing moose's head, not the penguin, and Wallace found himself at the back of the train once more. Only now Feathers had detached the engine and switched the carriages onto a branch line – *which ran out of track after a few feet!*

It looked like all was lost until Gromit grabbed a box of spare track and laid it down with lightning speed, taking the carriages back into the race. Under a table they went, directly across the line Feathers was on. Wallace made a grab for him, but caught the engine instead. The coal tender began to slow down.

'He's all yours, Gromit!' shouted Wallace, and Gromit reached out to catch the thieving bird. But he hadn't reckoned with the Techno-trousers. They entered the fray at just that moment and Feathers McGraw hit them, flying up into the air in a slow, graceful arc.

Gromit crashed into some kitchen cabinets and caught a milk bottle as it tumbled off the worktop. Feathers landed, as only a penguin could, right in the bottle. The diamond dropped neatly into Gromit's left paw. The chase was over.

Once Feathers McGraw was back safely behind bars and Wallace had collected the reward, there was nothing left to do but go home and have a nice cup of tea and some cheese and crackers.

'No more debts, eh, Gromit. And no more lodgers – more trouble than they're worth!' beamed Wallace, popping a cracker in his mouth. 'All's well that ends well, that's what I say – mmmm! I *do* like a bit of Gorgonzola!'

Gromit nodded and went back to reading the evening paper. Outside, the Techno-trousers, somehow knowing they weren't wanted any more, clanked away down West Wallaby Street and off into the setting sun.

First published by BBC Children's Books 1994
a division of BBC Enterprises Limited, Woodlands, 80 Wood Lane, London W12 OTT
Text by Graham Marks © 1994 BBC Children's Books,
Based on an original script by Nick Park and Bob Baker
Design by Richard White © 1994 BBC Children's Books
Stills taken from *The Wrong Trousers* © 1993 Wallace and Gromit Limited/BBC Enterprises Ltd
Wallace & Gromit ™ Wallace & Gromit Ltd, a member of the Aardman Animations group of companies
ISBN 0 563 40385 3
Printed and bound in Belgium by Proost NV
Colour separations by DOT Gradations, Chelmsford